Y0-DUH-401

by Wright Morris

NOVELS

In Orbit (1967)
One Day (1965)
Cause For Wonder (1963)
What A Way To Go (1962)
Ceremony In Lone Tree (1960)
Love Among The Cannibals (1957)
The Field Of Vision (1956)
The Huge Season (1954)
The Deep Sleep (1953)
The Works Of Love (1952)
Man And Boy (1951)
The World In The Attic (1949)
The Man Who Was There (1945)
My Uncle Dudley (1942)

PHOTO-TEXT

God's Country And My People (1968)
The Home Place (1948)
The Inhabitants (1946)

ESSAYS

A Bill Of Rites, A Bill Of Wrongs, A Bill Of Goods (1968)
The Territory Ahead (1958)

ANTHOLOGY

Wright Morris: A Reader (1970)

wright morris

GREEN GRASS,
BLUE SKY,
WHITE HOUSE

black sparrow press

los angeles

1970

LEE COUNTY LIBRARY
SANFORD, N. C.

Copyright © 1970
by Wright Morris

BLACK SPARROW PRESS
P. O. Box 25603
Los Angeles, California 90025

SBN 87685-067-0 (paper)
SBN 87685-068-9 (signed cloth)

Acknowledgement is hereby given to Harper's for *Since When Do They Charge Admission;* to Esquire for *Drrdla;* and to The New Yorker for *Green Grass, Blue Sky, White House.*

CONTENTS

SINCE WHEN DO THEY CHARGE ADMISSION

On the morning they left Kansas, May had tuned in for the weather and heard of the earthquake in San Francisco, where her daughter, Janice, was seven months pregnant. So she had called her. Her husband, Vernon Dickey, answered the phone. He was a native Californian so accustomed to earthquakes he thought nothing of them. It was the wind he feared.

"When I read about those twisters," he said to May, "I don't know how you people stand it." He wouldn't believe that May had never seen a twister till she saw one on TV, and that one in Missouri.

"Ask him about the riots," Cliff had asked her.

"What riots, Mrs. Chalmers?"

It was no trouble for May to see that Janice could use someone around the house to talk to. She was like her father, Cliff, in that it took children to draw her out. Her sister, Charlene, would talk the leg off a stranger but the girls had never talked much to each other. But now they would, once the men got out of the house. It had been Cliff's idea to bring Charlene along since she had never been out of Kansas. She had never seen an ocean. She had never been higher than Estes Park.

On their way to the beach, Charlene cried, "Look! Look!" She pointed into the sunlight; May could see the light shimmering on the water.

"That's the beach," said Janice.

"Just *look*," Charlene replied.

"You folks come over here often?" asked Cliff.

"On Vernon's day off," replied Janice.

9

"If it's a weekday," said May, "you wouldn't find ten people on a beach in Merrick County."

"You wouldn't because there's no beach for them to go to," said Janice.

Cliff liked the way Janice spoke up for California, since that was what she was stuck with. He didn't like it, himself. Nothing had its own place. Hardly any of the corners were square. All through the Sunday morning service he could hear the plastic propellers spinning at the corner gas station, and the loud bang when they checked the oil and slammed down the hood. Vernon Dickey took it all in his stride, the way he did the riots.

Janice said, "Vernon's mother can't understand anybody who lives where they have dust storms."

"I'd rather see it blow than feel it shake," said Cliff.

"Ho-ho!" said Vernon.

"I suppose it's one thing or another," said May. "When I read about India I'm always thankful."

Cliff honked his horn at the sharp turns in the road. The fog stood offshore just far enough to let the sun shine yellow on the beach sand. At the foot of the slope the beach road turned left through a grove of trees. Up ahead of them a chain, stretched between two posts, blocked the road. On the left side a portable contractor's toilet was brightly painted with green and yellow flowers. A cardboard sign attached to the chain read, *Admission 50¢.*

"Since when do they charge admission?" Janice asked. She looked at her husband, a policeman on his day off. As Cliff stopped the car a young man in the booth put out his head.

"In heaven's name," May said. She had never seen a man with such a head of hair outside of *The National Geographic.*

He had a beard that seemed to grow from the hair on his chest. A brass padlock joined the ends of a chain around his neck.

"How come the fifty-cent fee?" said Vernon. "It's a public beach."

"It's a racket," said the youth. "You can pay it or not pay it." He didn't seem to care. At his back stood a girl with brown hair to her waist, framing a smiling, vacant, pimpled face. She was eating popcorn; the butter and salt greased her lips.

"I don't know why anyone should pay it," said May. "Cliff, drive ahead."

Cliff said, "You like to lower the chain?"

When the boy stepped from the booth he had nothing on but a jockstrap. The way his plump buttocks were tanned it was plain that was all he was accustomed to wear. He stooped with his backside toward the car, but the hood was between him and the ladies. As the chain slacked Cliff drove over it, slowly, into the parking lot.

"What in the world do you make of *that?*" asked May.

"He's a hippie," said Janice. "They're hippies."

"Now I've finally seen one," said May. She twisted in the seat to take a look back.

"Maybe they're having a love-in down here," said Vernon, and guffawed. Cliff had never met a man with a sense of humor that stayed within bounds.

"Park anywhere," said Janice.

"You come down here alone?" asked May.

Vernon said, "Mrs. Chalmers, you don't need to worry. They're crazy but they're not violent."

Cliff maneuvered between the trucks and cars to where the front wheels thumped against a driftwood log. The sand began there, some of it blowing in the offshore breeze. The tide had washed up a sandbar, just ahead, that concealed the beach and most of the people on it. Way over, maybe five or ten miles, was the coastline just west of the Golden Gate, with the tier on tier of houses that Cliff knew to be Daly City. From the bridge, on the way over, Vernon had pointed it out. Vernon and Janice had a home there, but they wanted something more out in the open, nearer the beach. As a matter of fact, Cliff had come up with the idea of building them something. He was a builder. He and May lived in a house that he had built. If Vernon would come up with the piece of land, Cliff would more or less promise to put a house on it. Vernon would help him on the weekends, and his days off.

"What about a little place over there," said Cliff, and wagged his finger at the slope near the beach. Right below it were the huge rocks black as the water, but light on their tops. That was gull dung. One day some fellow smarter than the rest would make roof tiles or fertilizer out of it.

"Most of the year it's cold and foggy," said Vernon, "too cold for the kids."

"What good is a cold, windy beach?" said May. She had turned to take the whip of the wind on her back. No one answered her question. It didn't seem the right time to give it much thought. Cliff got the picnic basket out of the rear and tossed the beach blanket to Vernon. There was enough sand in it, when they shook it, to blow back in his face.

"Just like at home," Cliff said to Vernon, who guffawed.

Vernon had been born and raised in California, but he had got his Army training near Lubbock, Texas, where the dust still blew. Now he led off toward the beach, walking along the basin left where the tide had receded. Charlene trailed along behind him wearing the flowered pajama suit she had worn since they left Colby, on the fourth of June. They had covered twenty-one hundred and forty-eight miles in five days and half of one night, Cliff at the wheel. Charlene could drive, but May didn't feel she could be trusted on the interstate freeways, where they drove so fast. There was a time, every day, about an hour after lunch, when nothing Cliff could think or do would keep him from dozing off. He'd jerk up when he'd hear the sound of gravel or feel the pull of the wheel on the road's shoulder. Then he'd be good for a few more miles till it happened again. The score of times that happened Cliff might have killed them all but he couldn't bring himself to pull over and stop. It scared him to think of the long drive back.

"Except where it was green, in Utah," said May, "it's looked the same to me since we left home."

"Mrs. Chalmers," said Vernon, "you should've sat on the other side of the car."

It was enlightening to Cliff, after all he'd heard about the population explosion, to see how wide open and empty most of the country was. In the morning he might feel he was all alone in it. The best time of day was the forty miles or so he got in before breakfast. They slipped by so easy he sometimes felt he would just like to drive forever, the women in the car quiet until he stopped for food. Anything May saw before she had her coffee was lost on her. After breakfast Cliff didn't know what seemed longer: the day he put in waiting for the dark, or the long night he put in waiting for the light. He had forgotten about trains until they had to stop for the night.

Vernon said, "I understand that when they take the salt out of the water there'll be no more water problems. Is that right, Mr. Chalmers?"

Like her mother, Charlene said, "There'll just be others."

13

Was there anything Cliff had given these girls besides a poor start? He turned to see how Janice, who was seven months pregnant, was making out. The way her feet had sunk into the sand she was no taller than her mother. With their backsides to the wind both women looked broad as a barn. One day Janice was a girl — the next day you couldn't tell her from her mother. That part of her life that she looked old would prove to be the longest, but seem the shortest. Her mother hardly knew a thing, or cared, about what had happened since the war. The sight of anything aging, or anything just beginning, like that unborn child she was lugging, affected Cliff so strongly he could wet his lips and taste it. Where did people get the strength to do it all over again? He turned back to face the beach and the clumps of people who were sitting around, or lying. One played a guitar. A wood fire smoked in the shelter of a few smooth rocks. Vernon said, "It's like the coast of Spain." Cliff could believe it might well be true: it looked old and bleak enough. Where the sand was wet about half a dozen dogs ran up and down, yapping like kids.

"Dogs are fun! They just seem to know almost everything." This side of Charlene made her good with her kids, but Cliff sometimes wondered about her husband.

"How's this?" said Vernon, taking Cliff by the arm, and indicated where he thought they should spread the blanket. On one side were two boys, stretched out on their bellies, and nearer at hand was this blanket-covered figure, his back humped up. His problem seemed to be that he couldn't find a spot in the sand to his liking. He squirmed a good deal. Now and then his backside rose and fell. Cliff took one end of the blanket and Vernon the other, and they managed to hold it against the wind, flatten it to the sand. Charlene plopped down

14

on it to keep it from blowing. It seemed only yesterday that Cliff and his father would put her in a blanket and toss her like a pillow, scaring her mother to death. Charlene was one of those girls who was more like a boy in the way nothing fazed her. Out of the water, toward Vernon, a girl came running so wet and glistening she looked naked.

"Look at that!" said Cliff, and then stood there, his mouth open, looking. She was actually naked. She ran right up and passed him, her feet kicking wet sand on him, then she dropped to lie for a moment on her face, then roll on her back. Only the gold-flecked sand clung to her white belly and breasts. Grains of sand, cinnamon colored, clung to her prominent, erectile nipples. Her eyes were closed, her head tipped to the left to avoid the wind. For a long moment Cliff gazed at her body as if in thought. When he blinked his eyes the peculiar thing was that he was the one who felt in the fishbowl. Surrounded by them. What did they think of a man down at the beach with all his clothes on? He was distracted by a tug on the blanket and turned to see Vernon pointing at the women. They waddled along like turtles. All he could wonder was what had ever led them to come to a beach. Buttoned at the collar, Janice's coat draped about her like a tent she was dragging. Cliff just stood there till they came along beside him, and May put out a hand to lean on him. Sand powdered her face.

"It's always so windy?" she asked Vernon.

"You folks call this windy?" May looked closely at him to see if he meant to be taken seriously. He surely knew, if he knew anything, that she knew more about wind than he did.

"Get Cliff to tell you how it blows around Chadron," she said. "It blows the words right out of your mouth, if you'd let

15

it." Cliff was silent, so she added, "Don't it Cliff?"

"Don't it what?" he answered. He allowed himself to turn so that his eyes went to the humped squirming figure, under the blanket. The humping had pulled it up so the feet were uncovered. Four of them. Two of them were toes down, with tar spots on the bottoms: two of them were toes up, the heels dipped into the sand. In a story Cliff had heard but never fully understood, the point had hinged on the four-footed monster. Now he got the point.

"Blow the words right out of your mouth if you'd let it," said May. At a loss for words, Cliff moved to stand so he blocked her view. He took a grip on her hands and let her sag, puffing sour air at him, down to the blanket. "It's hard enough work just to get here," she said, and raised her eyes to squint at the water. "Charlene, you wanted to see the ocean: well, there it is."

Cliff was thinking that Charlene looked no older than the summer she was married. It was hard to understand her. She had had three children without ever growing up.

"If I'd known the sand was going to blow," said May, "we'd have stayed home to eat, then come over later. I hate sand in my food. Charlene, you going to sit down?"

Charlene stood there staring at a girl up to her ankles in the shallow water. She stooped to hold a child pressed to her front, the knees buckled up as if she squeezed it. A stream of water arched from the slit between the child's legs. The way she held it, pressed to her front, was like squeezing juice from a bladder. There was nothing Cliff could do but wait for it to stop. Charlene's handbag dangled to where it almost dragged in the sand.

"That's Farrallon Island," said Vernon, pointing. Without

his glasses Cliff couldn't see it. Janice tipped forward, as far as she could, to cup handfuls of sand over her ankles: she couldn't reach her feet. "We hear and read so much about their being so dirty," said May.

"It's the hippies," said Vernon. "They've taken it over."

Why was he such a fool as to say so? Even Cliff, who knew what he would see, twisted his head on his neck and looked all around him. The stark naked girl had dried a lighter color: she didn't look so good. The sand sprinkled her like brown sugar, but the mole-colored nipples were flat on her breasts, like they'd been snipped off. At her feet, using her legs as a backrest, a lank-haired boy, chewing blow-gum, sunned his pimpled face. On his hairless chest someone had painted his nipples to look like staring eyes. Now that Cliff was seated it was plainer than ever what was going on under the blanket: the heels of two of the feet thrust deep into the sand, piling it up. Cliff felt the eyes of Janice on the back of his head, but he missed those of her mother. Where were they?

"Cliff," she said.

He did not turn to look.

"Cliff," she repeated.

At the edge of the water a dappled horse galloped with two long-haired naked riders. If one was a boy, Cliff couldn't tell which was which.

"Who's ready for a beer?" asked Vernon, and peeled the towel off the basket. When no one replied he said, "Mr. Dickey, have yourself a beer," and took one. He moved the basket of food to where both Cliff and the women could reach it. Along with the bowl of potato salad there were two broiled chickens from the supermarket. The chickens were still warm.

"All I've done since we left home is eat," Cliff said.

17

"We just ate," said Janice.

"We didn't drag all this stuff here," said Cliff, "just to turn around and drag it back." He took out the bowl of salad. He fished around in the basket for the paper cups and plates. He didn't look up at May until he knew for certain she had got her head and eyes around to the front. The sun glinted on her glasses. Absent-mindedly she raked her fingers across her forehead for loose strands of hair. "We eat the salad first or along with the chicken?"

None of the women made any comment. One of the maverick beach dogs, his coat heavy with sand, stood off a few yards and sniffed at the chicken. "They shouldn't allow dogs on a beach," said Cliff. "They run around and get hot and can't drink the water. In the heat they go mad."

"There's salt in there somewhere," said Janice. "I don't put all the salt I could on the salad."

Cliff took out one of the chickens, and using his fingers pried the legs off the body. He then broke the drumsticks off the thighs, and placed the pieces on one of the plates.

"You still like the dark meat?" he said to Charlene. She nodded her head. He peeled the plastic cover off the potato salad and forked it out on the paper plates. "Eat it before the sand gets at it," he said, and passed a plate to May. Janice reached to take one, and placed it on the slope of her lap. Vernon took the body of one of the birds, tore off the wings, and tossed one to the dog.

"I can't stand to see a dog watch me eat," he said.

"Vernon was in Korea for a year," said Janice.

Cliff began to eat. After the first few swallows it tasted all right. He hadn't been hungry at all when he started, but now he ate like he was famished. When he traveled all he seemed to do was sit and eat. He glanced up to see that they were all eating except for May, who just sat there. She had her head cocked sidewise as if straining to hear something. Not twenty yards away a boy plucked a guitar but Cliff didn't hear a sound with the wind against him. Two other boys, with shorts on, one with a top on, lay out on their bellies with their chins in their hands. One used a small rock to drive a short piece of wood into the sand. It was the idle sort of play Cliff would expect from a kid about six, not one about twenty. On the sand before them a shadow flashed and eight or ten feet away a bird landed, flapping its wings. Cliff had never set eyes on a bigger crow. He was shorter in the leg but as big as the gulls that strutted on the firm sand near the water. A little shabby at the tail, big glassy hatpin eyes. Cliff watched him dip his beak into the sand like one of those glass birds that go on drinking water, rocking on the perch. One of the boys said, "Hey, you, bird, come here!" and wiggled a finger at him. When the bird did just that Cliff couldn't believe his eyes. He had a stiff sort of strut, pumping his head, and favored one leg more than the other. No more than two feet away from the heads of those boys he stopped and gave them a look. Either one of them might have reached out and touched him. Cliff had never seen a big, live bird as tame as that. The crows around Chadron were smarter than most people and had their own meetings and cawed crow language. They had discussions. You could hear them decide what to do next. The boy with the rock held it out toward him and damn if the crow didn't peck at it. Cliff could hear the click of his beak tapping the rock. He turned to see if May had caught that, but her eyes were on the plate in her lap.

"May, look—" he said.

Her eyes down, she said, "I've seen all I want to see the rest of my life."

"The crow—" said Cliff, and took another look at him. He had his head cocked to one side, like a parrot, and his beak clamped down on one of the sticks driven into the sand. He tried to wiggle it loose as he tugged at it. He braced his legs and strained back like a robin pulling a worm from a hole. So Vernon wouldn't miss it, Cliff put out his hand to nudge him. "Well, I'll be damned," Vernon said.

Two little kids, one with a plastic pail, ran up to within about a yard of the bird, stopped and stared. He stared right back at them. Who was to say which of the two looked the strangest. The kids were naked as the day they were born. One was a boy. Whatever they had seen before they had never seen a crow that close up.

"Come on, bird," said the boy with the rock, and waved it. Nobody would ever believe it, but that bird took a tug at the stick, then rocked back and cawed. He made such a honk the kids were frightened. The little girl backed off and giggled. The crow clamped his beak on the stick again and had another try. A lanky-haired hippie girl, just out of the water, ran up and said, "Sam — are they teasing you Sam?" She had on no top at all but a pair of blue-jean shorts on her bottom. "Come on bird!" yelled the boy with the rock, and pounded his fists on the sand. That crow had figured out a way to loosen up the stick by clamping down on it, hard, then moving in a circle, like he was drilling a well. He did that twice, then he pulled it free, clamped one claw on it, and cawed. "Good bird!" said the boy, and tried to take it from him, but that crow wouldn't let him. He backed off, flapped his wings, and soared off with his legs dangling. Cliff could see what it took a big bird like that to fly.

"What does he do with it?" said the girl. She looked off toward the cliffs where the bird had flown. Somewhere up there he had a lot of sticks: no doubt about that.

"Buries it," said the boy. "He thinks it's a bone."

The little girl with the plastic pail said, "Why don't you give him a real bone, then?" The boy and girl laughed. The hippie girl said, "Can I borrow a comb?" and the boy replied, "If you don't get sand in it." He moved so he could reach the comb in his pocket, and stroked it on his sleeve as he passed it to her. Combing her hair, her head tipped back, Cliff might have mistaken her for a boy. The little girl asked, "When will he do it again?"

"Soon as he's buried it," said the boy.

Cliff didn't believe that. He had watched crows all his life, but he had never seen a crow behave like that. He wanted to bring the point up, but how could be discuss it with a girl without her clothes on?

"Here he comes," said the boy, and there he was, his shadow flashing on the sand before them. He made a circle and came in for a landing on the firm sand. What if he did bury those sticks? His beak was shiny yellow as a banana. "Come here, bird!" said the boy, and held out the rock, but the girl leaned forward and grabbed it from him.

"You want to hurt him?" she cried. "Why don't you give him a real bone?" She looked around as if she might see one, raking the sand with her hands.

"Here's one, Miss!" said Cliff, and held the chicken leg out toward her. He could no more help himself than duck when someone took a swing at him. On her hands and knees the girl crawled toward him to where she could reach it. Her lank hair framed her face.

"There's meat on it," she said.

"Don't you worry," said Cliff, "crows like meat. They're really good meat eaters."

She looked at him closely to see how he meant that. About her neck a fine gold-colored chain dangled an ornament. Cliff saw it plainly. Two brass nails were twisted to make some sort of puzzle. She looked at the bone Cliff had given her, the strip of meat on it, and turned to hold it out to the bird. He limped forward like he was trained and took it in his beak. Cliff caught his eye, and what worried him was that he might want to crow over it and drop it. He didn't want him to drop it and have to gulp down sandy meat. But that bird actually knew he had something unusual since he didn't put it down to clamp his claws on it. Instead he strutted. Up and down he went, like a sailor with a limp. Vernon laughed so hard he gave Cliff a slap on the knee. "Don't laugh *at* him," said the girl, and when she put out her hand he limped toward her to where she could touch him, stroking with her fingers the flat top of his head. The little boy suddenly yelled and ran around them in a circle, kicking up sand, and hooting. The crow took off. The heavy flap of his wings actually stirred the hair of the boy who was lying there, nearest to him; he raised one of his hands to wave as the bird soared away.

"I never seen anything like it!" said Vernon.

"Maybe you'd like to come oftener." Janice picked at the bread crumbs in her lap.

"Did you see him?" asked Cliff. "You get to see him?"

"We can go now if you men have eaten." May made a wad of the napkin and scraps in her lap, put them under the towel and plates in the basket.

22

Vernon said, "Honey, you see that crazy bird?"

Janice shaded her eyes with one hand, peered at the sky. Up there, high, a bird was wheeling. Cliff took it for a gull. The wind had caked the color she had put on her lips, and sand powdered the wrinkles around her eyes. Cliff remembered they were called crow's feet, which was how they looked. Now she lowered her hand and held it out to Vernon to pull her up. The sand caught up in the folds of her dress blew over May and the girl lying behind her, one arm across her face.

"People must be crazy to come and eat on a beach," said May.

Cliff pushed himself to his feet, sand clinging to his chicken-sticky fingers. He helped Vernon with the blanket, walking toward the water where they could shake it and not disturb people. A bearded youth without pants, but with a striped T-shirt, sat with crossed legs at the edge of the water. The horse that had galloped off to the south came galloping back with just one rider on it. Cliff could see it was a girl. Janice and her mother had begun the long walk back toward the car. Along the way they passed the naked girl, still sprawled on her back.

"She's going to get herself a sunburn," said Vernon.

To Charlene Cliff said, "You see that bird?" Charlene nodded. "Just remember you did, when I ask you. Nobody back in Chadron is going to believe me if you don't."

"What bird was it?" asked May.

"A crow," said Cliff.

"I would think you'd seen enough of crows," said May.

At the car Cliff turned for a last look at the beach. The tide had washed up a sort of reef so that he could no longer see the water. The girl and the dogs that ran along it were like black paper cutouts. Nobody would know if she had her clothes on or off. He had forgotten to check on the two of them who had been squirming under the blanket. One still lay there. The other one crouched with lowered head, as if reading something. From the back Cliff wouldn't know which one was the girl.

May said, "I've never before really believed it when I said that I can't believe my eyes, but now I believe it."

"You wouldn't believe them if you'd seen that crow," said Cliff.

"I didn't come all this way to look at a crow," she replied.

They all got into the car, and Cliff put the picnic basket into the rear. He took a moment, squinting, to see if the crazy bird had come back for more bones. If he had just thought, he would have given the girl the other two legs to feed him.

"I'd like a cup of coffee," said May, "but I'm willing to wait till we get home for it."

Vernon said, "Mr. Chalmers, you like me to drive?" Cliff agreed that he would. They went out through the gate where they had entered but the boy and the girl had left the booth. The chain was already half-covered with drifting sand.

"It's typical of your father," said May, "to drive all the way out here and look at a crow."

Charlene said, "Wait until I tell Leonard!" They looked to see what she would tell him. On the dry slope below them a small herd of cattle were being fed from a hovering helicopter. Bundles of straw were dropped to spread on the slope.

"If I were you," said May, "I'd tell him about *that* and nothing else."

Cliff felt his head wagging. He stopped it and said, "Charlene, now you tell him about that crow. What's a few crazy people to one crow in a million?"

There was no comment.

"We're going up now," said Vernon. "You feel that poppin' in your ears?"

DRRDLA

The house needed painting when the Fechners acquired it, and Walter rented the equipment necessary to do it, climbing like a fireman to get at the rafters high in the gables. Inside, both the floors and the woodwork had been covered with many coats of paint. Walter removed it all to bring out the natural beauty of the wood. Light streamed through all of the high first-floor windows that Walter had cleaned with professional equipment. Whatever Walter undertook to do, he did professionally. In three of the upstairs rooms he installed cypress paneling obtained for a song from a demolition company, at the same time installing insulation materials that kept the summer heat out, the winter heat in. So much for first things first. In the dark months of the winter he taught himself to paint — among other things grinding his own colors — and with his wife Hanna's assistance, he took up the study of the cello. If it was largely a matter of application, Walter knew how to apply himself. He did no more than what he could, provided the day was long enough.

Hanna had "found" him in a jeweler's shop in Kussnacht, directly across the lake from Lucerne. His job had been to polish the silver and keep hundreds of cuckoo clocks cuckooing. They covered one solid wall of the shop into which Hanna had stepped to buy herself a new watchband, the pendulums rocking, the birds cuckooing, in one insane instant happening. The sight had so affected Hanna she had closed her eyes. Walter had spoken to her. Then another year passed before she returned, having made up her mind it was Walter she wanted.

One could hardly believe that to look at Hanna, a scholarly,

29

shy-seeming, very Swiss woman. It had been her decision. Perhaps her being older than Walter persuaded him to let her make it. He was so very much the man Hanna knew that she wanted, it was not necessary for her to be his ideal woman. That proved to be acceptable to Walter because women were not one of his major interests. He liked them, but he didn't need them. What he proved to need, after six years of marriage, was an intelligent, congenial male companion. That was Herman Lewin. He had been recruited with this in mind. Lewin badly needed a place to stay while he completed his medical studies. Walter's knowledge of German was a help to Lewin, and he in turn tutored Walter in the new analytic psychology. If the war came up, as it sometimes did, it was discussed in an open, intelligent manner. Herman Lewin was Jewish. Hanna and Walter Fechner were German-Swiss. They were all agreed that German culture could not be held responsible for a few madmen, anymore than all Americans could be held responsible for Huey Long.

"I tell you what," Hanna would say, lowering her cup with a clack to her saucer. "You men are all crazy. It's a *man's* crazy world." Hanna simply couldn't help, on occasion, showing her resentment for a man-run world. In Switzerland a woman did not have the right to vote, no matter how smart she was. In America she could teach, but not look forward to the usual promotions. A doddering idiot could head the department of German literature — as he now did — if his sex was male.

Hanna was not the lighthearted, uncomplicated person that Lewin had assumed from their exchange of letters. She had her moods. They made her, surely, more interesting. Like the night-light at the top of the stairs, she was either turned on, or she was turned off. Her work at the college demanded all of her strength, and she turned on for the college as she closed the door of the house behind her, and walked down the steps. In the way she strode off, carrying her stuffed valise, Lewin recognized the European in exile. Her pride and status tipped her slightly backward. The American who walked behind tipped slightly forward, forging ahead. In the late afternoon Hanna's return to the house was signaled by a loud clapping of her hands. A professor might do that to waken sleeping pupils. In this way Hanna summoned Walter and Lewin to tea. She would have changed her dress, and her face would be free of the light touch of makeup she wore to college. The tea hour permitted Hanna to enjoy at home some of the pleasures of supervision that were part of teaching. It was Hanna who spooned the tea from the pewter canister: Hanna who timed the steeping: and Hanna who poured — glancing up to check with Lewin, who sometimes varied, as to the number of lumps of sugar he wanted. Walter was allowed to slice up the küchen. Hanna judged the strength of the tea by its odor, an exercise that left a film of steam on her glasses. Much of this vexed Walter. To avoid the fuss, he might not appear until his tea was poured and cooling. An unsuspected side of Hanna's nature was revealed in the way she attacked her food. As if famished. Utterly absorbed until she was fed. Her way of opening her mouth, wide, then closing it with a bird-like chomp was disturbing. Later, with a finger moistened at her lips, she would peck around the table picking up crumbs, scraps of nuts, cake and icing. Into her appetite Hanna put a great deal of living. The strong brew of tea gave her pale face a flush and started, as she said, "her motor running." As a rule it would run for about two hours. This animated Hanna was

31

LEE COUNTY LIBRARY
SANFORD, N. C.

capable of "glee" — something new in Lewin's experience. She would give herself over, quite completely, to the humor of something Lewin had mentioned, not infrequently placing her hand on his arm, or as high as his shoulder, and applying astonishing pressure. The violin, she said, had done much to strengthen her hands.

Whatever Hanna believed to be so funny was invariably lost on Walter. He would sit waiting for her fit of humor to pass. Loose strands of her hair would cling to her lips, and tears of glee give a shine to her eyes. "If it's so amusing," Walter would say, "I fail to understand why you can't explain it." That she couldn't, of course, was what she found so amusing, and made matters worse. Minutes after such a scene at the table she might be heard giggling at the sink in the kitchen, or almost choking with laughter in her study. Walter put it down as a characteristic female symptom. Women were strange creatures, in Walter's opinion, still at the whimsical mercy of the moon's orbit. He detected, and complained of, the odor in the house during Hanna's "lunar period," during which time he took his shower in a stall he had erected in the basement. The basement smelled of nothing worse than fertilizer and hibernating plants.

Walter had a peasant's blunt directness of manner, but Lewin considered him rustically handsome. A woman might like him, although most objects were prone to bend or break in his hands. The handles snapped off cups, or broke off utensils, if Walter was asked to wash or dry them. His large-knuckled hands were those of a man half again his size. He broke off wine corks, snapped off pipestems, bent the prongs of forks as he mashed potatoes, and invariably cut so deep into the cheese board Lewin was warned to beware of splinters. In the basement, in fact, broken into fragments, were many mail-order objects he had tried to assemble. The iron legs of a new-type collapsible bed were twisted as if some monster had seized them. He snapped buttons off the collars of his shirts and the flies of his pants. It was of course impossible for him to shave without cutting himself. From the back and side his large knobby head resembled the Swiss carvings used for bottle stoppers, but his eyes were intelligent, and his voice, as a rule, pleasant. His gestures, however, in a heated discussion, were more like those of a karate expert, the flat of his hand slicing right or left, or brought down like a cleaver into his palm. It had not been easy for such a man to turn to painting, the cello, and the touch system of typing. The typing went the slowest, since the machine was usually in need of repair.

Walter's paintings were largely an excuse for making handsome frames. He drilled the wormholes by hand, and applied his own antique finish. These canvases were painted at the second-floor windows and demonstrated his mastery of perspective. No painting had been done out of the house. Walter did not like the curious gazing at him, or confusing him with some bohemian-type artist. All he was doing was showing what a man could do if he applied himself. He gave the pictures numbers, and signed himself Fechner where the signature was not obtrusive. He meant to say no more than that he was responsible for what he had made.

Lewin was still in bed, on a Sunday morning, when Walter rapped on his door. He came in with flecks of sawdust in his hair and a thick powder of the dust on his hands. It was common to see Walter Fechner heated—by work he did with his hands, or the warmth of his emotions—but Lewin had never before seen him excited. It changed the pitch of his voice.

He looked both foolish and appealing. "It's there!" he said.

Lewin said, "What?"

Walter shrugged in the European manner, spreading his hands.

"What is where?" Lewin repeated.

Walter replied. "The basement!" He spoke in a hushed, gruff whisper, as if someone were listening. Music thundered to a climax in Hanna's room. "It's there!" he said again, and Lewin was pleased to see, for himself, what Hanna had once seen in Walter. A boy's wide-eyed startled pleasure in a man's face. So what had happened? Walter had been at work at his bench, cutting a piece of glass. He had reached that stage where the glass had to be tapped with the tool to break it: a tingling sound is given off as it splinters. In the silence that followed this high-pitched vibration he heard this sound in the timbers behind him. That part of the basement was little more than an air space between the floor of the kitchen and the foundation. Old boards were piled there. Also a few traps in case of rats. There was no access to the basement from the yard, but Walter had found rat turds on his workbench. They were uncanny, those fellows. Walter had for them the highest respect.

His first thought was that he had caught a rat, and the creature, in pain, had made this sound. So he used a flashlight to check the traps back in the darkness. Both had been sprung, and the bait was gone. Otherwise nothing. He had stood there for some time, lost in thought. When he returned to work he picked up the glass and finished off what he had started. Once more, as the glass splintered, he had heard the sound. How describe it? Something between a peep and a squeak. So he took the trouble to clear away the boards and

34

aim the beam of the flashlight into the corners. At the farthest point, the way a distant road sign picks up the glint of the headlights, he saw—for a moment he saw—two eyes: glasslike splinters of chill went up and down his spine. The palm of the hand that gripped the light had filmed with sweat. The primeval, ur-fears of man needed only this spinal tingle to revive them. Eyes gleaming in a cavelike darkness. Sounds that were felt as much as they were heard.

What had Walter done? At the moment nothing. He had been paralyzed. Sometime later he had aimed the beam of spotlight into the darkest corner. Walter and this creature had just stared at each other. A bat, possibly? No, the head was too large. In Walter's experience it resembled the slender loris, a bizarre creature he had seen only in books. A head that appeared all eyes. Fearing to damage eyes so long accustomed to darkness Walter had switched off the light and come straight to Lewin. What did he want? What he wanted from Lewin was advice.

That he thought he would get it from Lewin was a measure of his confusion. Lewin's feeling about anything found in basements was not one of excitement. Why else had he picked an apartment in the attic if not to get as far as possible from basements? Anything that slithered, squirmed, or dragged a tail was not, for Lewin, an object of study. But that was not yet known. Whatever it was, it had not yet moved. Lewin's advice—since Walter stood there, waiting—was to lure the creature into the open. Put down food and water. Put down anything the poor devil might eat. In a picture magazine Lewin had once seen a beast all eyes and ears, like a giant Mickey Mouse.

"That's a loris," said Walter, and in that simple manner he

recovered his sense of proportion. It was not really advice he wanted or needed from Lewin—just his reassurance.

He did take Lewin's tip about the food, and put down samples of cheese, meat and nuts, and canned fish. Also cereals, dry and cooked. What happened? Nothing. Nor did it respond to the bait of warm milk. That would have settled the matter for Lewin, but it merely increased the challenge for Walter. He prepared more fish, both fresh and canned mackerel, and pushed the tin plate of food back into the darkness. The next morning he could see that the mackerel had been licked clean of the sauce. More sauce was added, and this too licked off. Was it only the sauce that it liked, or did it lack the strength, or the teeth, to chew with? Walter asked Lewin, whose teeth were not so good. So that the creature could gum the fish, if necessary, a pulpy soup was made of the mackerel. That helped. The loris proved to have a weakness for canned fish soup.

From the basement stairs, where Walter kept his vigil, he used mirrors to keep his eyes on the food plate. A dim, indirect light, from a shaded bulb, transformed the scene into a parched, barren landscape. In this tableau a rat would loom as large as a dinosaur. At its farthest rim, all ears and popped eyes, a creature gazed toward Walter with a fish-smeared snout, then turned, like a reptile, and squirmed off. The tail it dragged was thin and long as a rat's, but covered with fur. If Walter could believe his eyes he had seen a starved cat. Fortunately, for Lewin, he would have to wait until the creature had gained both courage and substance. This would take time. Lewin had to gain a little courage himself.

Walter began with liquid vitamins smeared on the fish or dropped into the saucer of canned milk. Quite simply, the creature had to learn to both chew food and digest it. Like a healthy cat choking on a fur ball, it had to swallow, and gag, then swallow again. Walter was patient. He spoke words of comfort and encouragement. In return it might make the sound suggested by the word drrdla, with a rolling of the r's. Not a mew, or a meow, but a sound that looked forward—as Walter put it—to being a real mew someday. Drrdla. For the moment it served as a name. If Walter made a move in its direction it would squirm like a reptile into the darkness, but if he made only coaxing, catlike noises it was not disturbed. When Lewin came down for breakfast he would find Walter on the basement stairs, off the landing, a flashlight in his lap and a pair of bird glasses on a strap about his neck.

"How's your friend?" Lewin would ask.

"She's coming," Walter would reply, although the matter of sex was still undetermined. Her color, from what he could tell, had once been grey and white.

What it all came down to, in Walter's opinion, was the emergence of life from darkness. God knows where the creature had come from, or what had been the cause of its terror, but it now slowly squirmed its way from the primeval past into the present. It had managed to live, like a hibernating plant, on snatches of light. The very idea of a friendly gesture, or an upward look, had not emerged into its consciousness. What Walter found on his hands was a creature, like man, that had fallen from Grace. Some blind or deliberate moment of terror had erased its mind of all experience. A *tabula rasa*. It had to begin, once more, from scratch. Would it be possible to restore such a fallen creature to normal life? If possible, Walter would do it. In that simple animal, as in man, there was a hunger for human affection: in its tiny, wounded soul it was drawn toward the light it feared. Like some people, it had lived in darkness so long it found the presence of light painful. The parallels were endless. The challenge inexhaustible. No project Walter had previously undertaken tested, at once, so many of his talents. Commitment and patience. Walter would prove to have what the challenge required. Every day he modified, in some way, the approach he used to win her over. It was the talk she liked: a very womanly aspect of her temperament. To enlarge his range Walter used a birdcall that employed a piece of metal in a wooden disk. What sounds he made! How her eyes would widen, her large, bat-like ears would twitch. This could be observed from the landing of the stairs without intruding on her privacy. Lewin observed it. A head (he did not say so) like those withered specimens on women's fur pieces, with gems for eyes. Hanna preferred to wait, as she said, until it looked more like a cat than a rodent. That would take time. Out of long habit the creature crawled rather than walked.

Just living in the dark had developed, in Drrdla, faculties that most cats had learned to do without. Her eyes, for example, were not to be trusted. She relied on other, subtler, signals. It was not out of the question that a room full of light would blind her as badly as total darkness. Take such a simple thing as perspective. How it was that objects, in *her* space, related to her. What was near and far, up and down. How high she could leap. How far she could fall. The blind woman, Helen Keller, had learned to live in a world that had no dimensions whatsoever. Drrdla was not so handicapped, but neither was she so smart. To make her way back to normal life she had to recover much of what she had lost, as well as discover faculties that were new to cats. If she made it, she would be a sort of cat-genius, starting from scratch. If one was fond of cats it could be depressing how dumb they were in simple situations, but it was inspiring what they could do when the going was tough. Few had ever had tougher going than Drrdla, if she proved to be tough enough.

The lyrical side of Walter's nature, not previously displayed, revealed a faculty that he had allowed to languish. Circumstance now required that he exercise it to an unusual degree, at breakfast. In these discussions Lewin had a glimpse of the rough diamond Hanna had plucked from the bed of cuckoo clocks. In these moments the knobheaded, iron-handed peasant underwent a transformation. Why not? Wasn't that just what he was pointing out? Evolution itself, he told Lewin, had surely come about in just this manner. This kind of thinking, of course, went around and around, and that was how Walter went. Around and around. Lewin watched and listened, sometimes risking what he felt to be a pertinent observation. What if this creature finally made it? Became a plain, normal cat. Both Hanna and Walter had once and for all decided not to be the victims of pets: it was pets that had people. It was pets that determined their lives. Wouldn't this cat, when it *lived* in the house, be some sort of pet? Walter said that such a prospect was so far away he hadn't given it serious consideration. One thing at a time. The thing at the moment was the basement wall.

This low cement wall, about waist-high, divided Drrdla's territory from the rest of the basement. She would come to the edge of it, no further, to nibble her fish. If Walter moved the plate to his workbench, or the floor, there it would sit through the night untouched. This wall, in short, provided her with the line that simplified decisions. From its edge she would crouch and exchange glances with Walter. What did he want? What did he now expect of *her*? This confronted Walter with a dilemma he was not in a position to answer. What *did* he want—besides just wanting her to come out? Suppose she really felt more at her ease with the life she had? Food enough, now, on the one hand: and all that privacy on the other. What—her glance seemed to ask—did he have in mind?

In Walter's opinion the problem was aggravated by the apparent increase of noise. Doors slammed. Was this something new, or had he merely not noticed it so much in the past? At his vigil in the basement these jarring blasts rattled the house like an earth tremor. Was it necessary? Hanna couldn't seem to gather what the trouble was. Had it reached the point, she asked, where entering and leaving her very own house created a disturbance? Would he like her to pad around the house barefoot, leaving her shoes at the door like a Japanese? Was it all right if she listened to music in the evening, or was awakened in the morning by her alarm? If just her living in the house disturbed his *little rodent*, perhaps she should think of taking a room elsewhere. Plainly, Walter and the cat couldn't, living, as they did, in such perfect harmony in the basement. Walter hardly knew which disturbed him more, the unpredictable and shattering slam of a door, or the tireless and deliberate way she referred to the creature as his "little rodent."

"How is Walter's little rodent?" she would ask Lewin, first making certain that Walter was within hearing. As aggravating, and even more of a nuisance, was the clattering ring of the phone. An especially loud ring had been installed so that it might be heard both upstairs and in the basement. The

40

cat was naturally startled by the ring, and the way Walter turned and ran up the stairs. What were these calls? He was often just a moment too late to hear. Other times Hanna would like to know if there was something *they* would like at the market, fish or liver, perhaps? What could Walter do? If he allowed his irritation to show, the phone would ring ten minutes later. Both Walter and Hanna had been insistent on having an unlisted number, but now he received calls from solicitors and pollsters. The telephone company could not help him. Hanna would not torment herself trying to learn a new number, after so many years of mastering the old one. To tell him *that*, she phoned.

There were other things: doors were left ajar so a draft would bang them; the thermostat was jiggled on the hot-water heater, resulting in explosive bangs in the heating system. Lewin tried to point out that Walter's suspicions, seen objectively, were without foundation. Doors often slammed; anyone with a phone was sometimes driven almost crazy by it. Circumstance—not Hanna—had made him just a wee bit paranoid. Living in the basement, all ears, like the cat, had given him the feeling that the house was against him. That was almost as silly as Hanna behaving in a jealous manner. Was she crazy?—Walter wanted to know. Jealous of a cat? Lewin suggested that both cats and women had this lunatic side to their natures. They were possessed, so to speak. They would eat or not eat, hide in the darkness or spend the night wailing. They were at once affectionate, trusting, and suspicious of every movement. Idio-cy ruled the world of men— the personal, the separate, the distinct, et cetera — while luna-cy permeated the world of women, their nature subject to forces, and impulses, not easily controlled.

A student of Hanna's, Emil Lubke, who majored in German literature and the piano, was given the key to the house so that he could practice on the idle Fechner piano. Did Walter mind? No, he was free to go for long walks. It took hours of patient, loving coaxing, however, to lure the poor cat, Drrdla, back to the light after two solid hours of Rachmaninoff and Liszt. She now accepted — possibly she even needed — the merest touch of his outstretched hand. Her posture was wary. The tremor in her legs was like that of a kitten with the rickets. All along her bony spine the hairs lifted, and her ears might flatten at the slightest disturbance. It was not unusual for her to cuff him, or with her fangs showing make the hiss of a dragon. This involuntary behavior embarrassed them both, but encouraged a fresh beginning. Palpable to his touch was the muted tremor of her purr. Another thing she couldn't help. The poor creature was torn, in Walter's opinion, between the two great forces that move the world—including the moon. The desire to open out, to confront what is new, and the fear that dictated withdrawal. Vulnerable. The deep fear of being vulnerable. Irresistibly she stretched toward Walter's hand, the mysterious gratification of his touch, and yet an equally compulsive force lured her back into the comforts of darkness. Walter dare not advance, nor make other moves associated with the food plate, but it was clear she *preferred*, after eating, completing her toilet while seated near him. If he remained, she would crouch and take her nap. A puzzling detail was that she always did this with her back to him, her head toward the darkness. Her ears carefully screened his movements, but it did seem a symbolic gesture. It was now Walter *and* Drrdla, against the unknown. Walter could therefore be excused the glance of witless delight he gave Lewin when she allowed him, in Lewin's presence, to scratch her ears. This silent colloquy brought to mind lovers otherwise speechless with emotion. Little wonder that Hanna never seemed to find the time to see how the pair of them were doing. Did she know? As well as she seemed to know the exact moment to startle them both out of their wits? At the electric moment that Walter's finger left the tingling chill of her nose—the phone would ring, a door would slam, or the pipes that ran along the basement ceiling would be convulsed with a pulsing throb, caused by the clever manipulation of the hot-water taps in the bathroom. If both were turned on suddenly, and full, the plumbing pounded like a sick monster. The cat, Drrdla, would disappear. Walter would sit there in the dark, his head in his hands.

If he continued to sit there long enough, however, he would hear, in the shelter of the steps, the drag of her tongue on a patch of her pelt, a sign that she had recovered and in no way held him responsible. He supplemented her diet with wheatgerm oil cunningly smeared on fresh chicken livers. She preferred canned milk to fresh cream, and liked nothing better than to gnaw on colossal-size non-pitted olives. She growled like a tiger when her teeth struck the stone. An olive rolled across the floor and caught her, so to speak, with her guard down. She leaped and pounced. Very peculiar behavior for a sick cat. Equally intimate and peculiar was her lust for the rind of a melon. Walter had left his breakfast slice on the step to gallop up the stairs and answer the phone: when he returned the rind had been chewed away at both ends. Other specialties included peanut butter, cream cheese on bagel, and cold matzo-ball soup. Anything but mice, was Hanna's comment. There *were* a few mice—they rustled wastebasket paper and ate the nuts out of the candy on Hanna's desk—but Walter pointed out this would be taken care of when Drrdla had the run of the house. The remark slipped out. He hadn't meant to go so far, so fast. Hanna made no comment, but a day later he found the basement door propped open. She picked the following weekend to repot most of her plants. This took all of Saturday, and with the racket and confusion Walter saw nothing at all of Drrdla. Hanna also filled the house with fall leaves and dried arrangements, the doors slamming as she went in and out, not to mention the search for bowls and containers in all corners of the basement. Walter himself took one of his long, joyless walks, a McIntosh apple swelling his pocket. Now and then he could hear, wind-borne, the roar of the crowd at the Army-Navy game. The lights were on in the house when he returned, and the door of the kitchen was still propped open. To air out the smell of fertilizer two kitchen windows were propped up from the bottom. Hanna lay soaking in the tub. Walter put out a fresh plate of food for the cat while he scrambled some eggs for himself. Eggs too she liked. But that night she touched nothing on her plate. Walter coaxed her for an hour, then he took the flashlight and probed the corners she usually retired to. Nothing doing. He went from room to room and from the top of the house to the bottom. He discussed the disappearance for some time with Lewin. However improbable, it was possible that she had come up the stairs to the kitchen and gone through the door or one of the windows. What else? Walter spent the evening circling the block. It was not one of those streets with alleys, so all he could do was stop and peer up the driveways, making those sounds that caused other cats to howl and strange dogs to bark.

The following day Walter moved a cot from the basement to the kitchen. If he heard a cat mewing at the door he would be there, handy, to let the creature in. Part of each night Walter might make a tour of the house. Lying there on the cot he would think of a closet, or some nook or cranny a cat might crawl into, and having thought of it he would have to get up and look. He came up with the bizarre idea that she might have gone up the fireplace. He felt it explained the sprinkle of soot he often heard at night. Naturally, it meant no more fires were started, and at night a dish of food was left on the hearth, just in case. How was one to know just where she might be, until she reappeared? The smell of fish permeated the house. Walter felt obliged to change it daily, making sure it was fresh.

Hanna complained to Lewin that Walter's prowling deprived her of sleep. Her own door she kept locked, with a rug at the bottom, unless she heard Lewin passing. On an equal-time basis, Lewin felt obliged to listen to her side of the story. That too was a long one. Hanna had grown thinner, or rather leaner, but it seemed more appropriate to her role. Her fingers were always nervously laced together, or gripping the arm or the back of a chair. When she spoke to Walter she would always get to her feet. With a chair between them—her hands gripping its back—she would read him one of her "lectures." She was relieved, she told him, that the poor little rodent had managed to escape. It was not being saved for itself at all, but was being held a captive creature by Walter. What the poor cat hungered for was not food, but the company of its own kind. If that was not true it would still be in the basement fattening on chicken liver and Wal-

45

ter's attention. What it wanted, and finally got, was a chance to escape.

Lewin very much admired the way Walter would sit and listen to Hanna as if he felt he had it coming. Walter said it did her good to "blow her top." He put in his time fencing off those areas in the basement where a cat might hide. The night the cat came home Hanna was in bed with a slight flu. Lewin went down alone to the door of the kitchen where he watched, unobserved, the shabby grey-and-white cat gulping up canned mackerel. Was it Drrdla? Spotted grey-and-white cats look pretty much alike. Her splotched white patches were uniformly soiled. Lewin seemed to recall the ears as larger, the tail longer and thinner, but in point of fact he had seldom seen her. His picture of the cat had been formed by Walter's numberless descriptions.

"It's her," Walter said, putting his finger to her head. "I can feel her mew." It was a fact that the cat proved to be curious about the basement, and seemed responsive to the name Drrdla. A final proof would have been a strip of melon rind, but melons were not in season. Walter had also stopped buying the large unpitted olives and had only the green ones, stuffed with pimentos, one of the few things she had tried to bury after sniffing it.

A place was prepared for the cat in the kitchen—a box for sleeping, and a litter box for business—but when Walter came down in the morning she was gone. He searched the house. The cat was finally found asleep at the foot of Hanna's unmade bed. After eating, it was back at her door, where it howled until it gained entrance. There it was when Hanna returned from school, and she thought nothing of it. "Hello, cat," she said. She was not surprised that so smart a cat would rather sleep with her than alone in the kitchen. Why not? It merely showed how sensible she was. The litter box was then moved to Hanna's room since the cat also preferred to spend the day there. The windows were warm and sunny. The place she loved to sleep was on old theme papers in Hanna's wastebasket. Nor did it come as a surprise to Hanna that the cat put on weight in an alarming manner, or chose the top drawer of her bureau—the one with old stockings—to bear and nurse a litter of four kittens, two of them black. During the long day Hanna was not in the room they could be heard doing what four kittens like to do. Walter was kept busy emptying the litter box, and trying to spade up frozen earth in the snow-covered garden. The names of the kittens were Eenie, Meenie, Miney and Moe. Miney and Moe were black. Hanna sometimes carried Moe to the college, in her muff, where he slept in her desk drawer, or played with an eraser. The mother cat, once her work was done, proved to be loose and immoral in her ways. She would howl from room to room, and from floor to floor, until Walter got up and let her out. A night or two later she would howl from door to door until he let her in. Why didn't Hanna complain? She seemed to think it perfectly normal behavior. Once a cat had learned what real life was like, what did Walter expect? Hadn't it been Walter's idea in the first place to help her to develop her faculties? To restore her to Grace? Like some people, she had lived in the darkness so long the light of day almost made her giddy. Hanna knew how she felt.

Hanna was scandalized when Walter brought up the idea of having the mother cat fixed. What would he think of next?—she wanted to know. He helped her weigh the cat on the bathroom scale for the first alarming signs of increase. At

47

LEE COUNTY LIBRAR
SANFORD, N. C.

that point she will need more riboflavin, as it says in the book. Walter was sometimes up four or five times a night letting her in, and then letting her out. It is perfectly plain she now abuses his concern: what can he do? The sound of his padding up and down the stairs keeps Lewin awake. For some time Lewin has been sleeping in a larger bed, and it is Hanna who lies there beside him. Sometimes she giggles. Other times she laughs hysterically. It was this sound that led Lewin to think she was sobbing, and why he opened the door to her room. She beckoned to him. Catlike, he proved open to suggestion. If a laughing fit comes on her late at night she controls it by pressing her face to her pillow. The howling of the Toms will bring a flood of laugh tears to her eyes. It is Hanna's back that Lewin feels he knows the best. After her pleasure, like a cat, she shows him her back. Lewin lets his fingers glide along her spine, which seems to him as bony as that of Drrdla, the fuzz of hair along it rising, the back arching, as when Walter first extended his hand toward the dark. If he had then withdrawn it, an unawakened, famished cat still would be captive in the basement, and neither Walter nor Lewin would have on their hands a female creature awakened to life.

GREEN GRASS, BLUE SKY, WHITE HOUSE

As I sit here, Floyd's mother mows the lawn. The whine of the mower can be heard above the noise of her grandchildren at their horseplay. If I close my eyes the sounds are like those we see in comic strips, WHAM! BAM! POWIE! rising in balloons, or exploding like firecrackers. All in fun, of course. They are healthly, growing animals and have to work off their energies somehow. Why not with the mower? Mrs. Collins likes to mow her own lawn. Any day but Sunday, either Franklin DeSpain, or Lyle, or even Melanie, would pop up from somewhere and do it for her, but Reuben DeSpain insists that his children keep the Sabbath holy. The Lord rested, and so do the DeSpains.

A farm girl to begin with, Mrs. Collins likes to get her hands on a machine that works and work it. The blades spin free when she nears a tree and uses short, choppy strokes. The whine of the mower makes its way around the house, and on the long run at the back it is almost gone. It stops when twigs from the elms catch between the blades. I can tell she likes to work around the tree trunks where the short, hard strokes set the blades to whirring. That's a sound from my boyhood. The whirring blades of a mower pushed by somebody else. I would wait for the thump as it hit the house at the end of its run. People in this country once might have been divided into those who knew that sound and those who didn't; those who liked it and those it made almost sick. All summer long, freshly cut lawn grass weighted the cuffs of my father's pants.

One of Franklin DeSpain's boys walks by with a skateboard he carries around looking for sidewalks. Not all the streets in

Ordway have them. The lawns slope down to bleed into the weeds, and the weeds into the crumbling blacktop. Most of the walks in town are of brick heaved into waves and troughs by tree roots. The only walking people do is from the door at the back of the house to the car parked in the drive.

The town of Ordway, in Missouri, is one where no line is drawn between what is rural and what is urban. A cow is tethered in the lot facing the square, where the sidewalk bristles with parking meters. I've seen no pigs, but the older residents, like Floyd's mother, keep a goat, or a cow, or a few fenced chickens. Everything is here to make the good life possible. Mrs. Collins at one point gave up the chickens but Mr. Collins missed their cackling. The silence disturbed his rest in the morning. If she forgets to collect the eggs, they soon have an old hen with a fresh batch of chicks. Almost an acre of lawn surrounds the house, and there is sometimes snow in the yard till Easter, the first spears of spring grass pale as winter wheat. At the back it's hard to tell where the lawn ends and the fields begin.

One thing I have learned is that small-town people have a pallor you can seldom find in the city. If they roll up a sleeve, or tuck up a pants leg, the bit of skin that shows is white as a flour sack. Mrs. Collins wears a pair of Floyd's unlaced tennis sneakers on her bare feet. His sweaters also fit her. Her overalls, however, once belonged to Mr. Collins, and the seat and knees are patched with pieces of quilting. That makes for more comfort when she kneels to weed, and less dampness when she sits to cut greens. A faded gingham sunbonnet sits back on her head to let the sun warm her face.

In the fall the yard is so bright with leaves Mrs. Collins tells me it's almost painful to look at. They have to pull the shades

52

at the windows to sleep at night. Both a fact of that sort or a death in the family Mrs. Collins reports with an appealing smile. If my eyes are on her face I often miss the gist of what she is saying. Her expression remains the same: a beaming smile, an affable, open good nature. If I hear her laughing, it is usually at herself. This can be disconcerting when it signals something is wrong. She laughed, her daughter tells me, when she fell and broke her hip. Of Scotch descent, with a long Quaker family background, Mrs. Collins believes "the slings and arrows of misfortunes," as she says, are as much to be experienced as anything else. Nothing has diminished her appetite for life.

The Collins house is *substantial,* as my father would have said, with a runaround porch that is tilted like a ship's deck, the spacious lawn shaded by sycamores and elms. There's a cleared spot at the back, hard as blacktop, where the trash and the leaves are burned. The two-board gap in the fence indicates a shortcut that connects the Collins house with the one across the alley. Her daughter Ruth lives there, but Ruth's three teen-age boys spend most of their time in the Collins kitchen, or roughhousing at the back of the yard. A trough is worn into the yard where a tire swings from the limb of an elm.

The Collins kitchen is big, and uncluttered with modern conveniences. Mrs. Collins makes my toast under the flame in the oven, then scrapes the char off at the sink. She does not believe in anything, as she says, "that you have to plug in." The crackle of her long hair, worn in a loose bun at her neck, is her daily assurance that her health is in order and her battery is charged. In the house she wears a simple grey frock with touches of faded lace at the wrists and throat. I've no idea if she knows how much it does for her corn-yellow hair. She prefers to stand, rather than sit, her hip inclined on the stove rail, or the sink, with one of her brown freckled hands holding a loose wad of her apron, cupped like a bird. She tests heat and flavor with her fingers, spits on the skillet before making hotcakes. Into the first pot of percolator coffee she puts a pinch of salt and one fresh eggshell, preferably white. I'm told that the house swarmed with cats until her daughter Ruth married and took most of them with her. Mrs. Collins says, "I don't mind having pets, but I don't like the pets having people," meaning Mr. Collins and his old dog Ruby, now dead three years. Every day in his life, which proved to be a long one, Ruby would walk Mr. Collins to the railroad crossing, look up and down in both directions, then lead him across if it was safe. When Mr. Collins stopped making the walk, Ruby went under the house porch and refused to come out. It was the end of the run for both Ruby and the St. Louis & Troy.

Although it is fifteen years since a train entered Ordway, Mr. Collins still wears the striped overalls preferred by trainmen, and one of the high-crowned, long-billed brakeman's hats. This he leaves on his head until Mrs. Collins says, "Papa, your cap." All members of the family speak of him as Papa, but not often to his face. His skin is smooth, as if dampened and then stretched on his skull. The abundance of his hair gives the impression that his head is not fully developed, or with time has shrunk. His pale blue eyes have a focus just beyond the object of his attention. Before speaking he nervously fingers the bill of his cap. The two subjects Mr. Collins never loses sight of are Norman Thomas and the old dog Ruby. A picture of Ruby, a gourd-shaped little terrier with his head almost swallowed by his thickening neck, is among the family portraits on the sewing machine. More recent snapshots, featuring the grandchildren, Waldo, Luther, and Clarence, are on the piano. Waldo and Luther take after their father, a huge, affable man in the road-construction business. The younger boy, Clarence, is small-boned like his mother, but almost six feet tall. He has grown too fast, and his movements are those of a boy on stilts. The boys like to roughhouse and can usually be heard clopping up and down the stairs of the Collins house, chased by Clarence, or mawling like dogs at the back of the yard. Waldo has picked up such lingo as "Sock it to me!" supplemented with cries of "Wham! Bam! Powie!" The trouble starts when Clarence, wearing one of Melanie's aprons, helps her wash and dry the dishes.

It is a point of pride with Mrs. Collins that she has no keys; the house is never locked. Back in the Depression, when they took in roomers, the keys disappeared in the pockets of strangers, and Mrs. Collin has never troubled to replace them. Mr. Collins pads through my room, while I sleep, because it has always been his way to the bathroom. If he took another route, strange to his habits, he might easily stumble or bump into something. To close a door so that it clicks is to imply that you have something to hide. It has been years since the bathroom door actually latched shut. If it is closed, the draft nudges it open. During the night the light provides a beacon, and the drip in the tub is like the tick of a clock. Unless the bathroom door stands open wide, it is safe to assume there is someone behind it. Most members of the family make a characteristic sound when steps approach. Mrs. Collins hums, Melanie turns on a faucet in the bowl and lets it run. Mr. Collins, however, is absolutely silent. He sits dreaming on the stool, his brown hands on his white knees, his gaze on the leaf-clogged gutters of the porch visible from the bathroom window. An intruder need not disturb him. The boys shower while he sits there. Privacy can be had by going up one floor and using the small water closet, but the flush of the water when the chain is pulled seems designed to clean out miles of plumbing, and burps in all the sinks.

If this were not Sunday, or if the grass had been mowed, Mrs. Collins would be seated in the porch rocker. It is of wood, the rungs turned by hand, the cane seat so new it resembles plastic. Layers of green and brown paint are visible where Mrs. Collins grips the chair arms. She takes a strong grip when she rocks, as if she feared the chair might take off. The spreading legs are reinforced with baling wire still fuzzy with the hair of the Collins cats. They used to retire there to get away from Ruby, and one of the toms had his tail amputated. Never again did he set foot on the Collins porch.

At one time as many as eight or ten children ran in and out of the house, and sagged the rails of the porches. The chain swing had to be taken down to keep them from wearing a hole in the clapboards. They *had* to rock it sideways, or swing it so high the whole house leaned one way, then the other. The hooks for the swing are still there in the ceiling, but who would swing if they put it back up? Not the new generation. The porch stoop used to sag with the DeSpain children, who were too polite to use the hammock. They were noisy, but they had breeding and refused to do a lick of work on Sunday. Mr. Collins would torment them by offering them money to run down and buy him his White Owl cigar. The other days of the week they had to offer to do it for nothing. For every biscuit that was eaten at the Collins table, two biscuits went out the door with Rosemary DeSpain, Reuben's wife, along with what she loosely defined as "leftovers." She in turn donated her coffee stamps during the war, when Mr. Collins began to suffer his withdrawal headaches. He was accustomed to eight strong cups a day, and that was what he got. Sunday being the day of rest, the DeSpains liked to spend it where they could watch other people work. Rosemary is gone now, but Mrs. Collins tells me she got up early to sit in the Collins kitchen, watching Ruth and Mrs. Collins prepare the Sunday meal. In case she ever had to do it, she wanted to be sure she knew how it was done.

Reuben DeSpain tells me that his wife was black and blue as a new stovepipe, but their children and grandchildren are best described as "golden oak." DeSpain claims that it comes from his French and Castilian ancestry. The boys have their father's light copper tan, but Melanie is so pale out-of-town people take her for an Italian, like Sophia Loren. She has Sophia's big, half-popped eyes and wide full mouth. Mrs. Collins likes to tell how Floyd would ask her why his own tan peeled and Melanie's didn't. Unless she smiles, or talks, her impassive expression appears to be sullen. Melanie is inclined to be accident-prone, and wears Band-Aids on her fingers and arms for stove burns. The burn soon heals, but the print of the adhesive leaves a visible pattern. Mrs. Collins says to her, "Melanie, that stove bite you again?" Melanie's chores are to cook, tidy up, make the beds, and hand-wash Floyd's dress shirts in case he dirties any. She leaves the ironing board standing, blocking the pantry, to show that a woman's work is never done. She smokes Camels as she works, dropping the ashes on the ironing and between the sheets.

"One day you're going to burn this house down," Mrs.

Collins says, and both women laugh. Melanie leaves the butts resting on the ashtrays, the edges of the bureaus, windowsills, and cereal cartons, or they slow-burn holes in the oilcloth or char a hole in the plastic soap dishes, or burn down till they tilt off something and drop to the floor. When Melanie laughs she turns her back and you see the top of her head rather than the roof of her mouth. She takes shame in her dark laughter, and wipes it off her mouth before she turns to face me. Around the house, as a dust cap, she wears a shower hat in which she stores her matches and pack of Camels. Thinking up things to keep Melanie "busy" is one of Mrs. Collins' endless chores. While Melanie wanders around tidying up, Mrs. Collins prepares for her the well-balanced lunch she never gets at home. Left to herself Melanie will eat nothing but creamed canned corn and chipped beef in a white sauce. She loves diet cola spiked with a spoonful of chocolate syrup. The two women eat together, discussing samples of cloth Mrs. Collins receives from a store in Chicago. She has in mind a dress for herself and a new winter coat for Melanie.

One of Floyd's chores, when he was at home, was to pick up Melanie in the morning and get her home to make her father's supper in the evening. On arriving, Melanie calls out, "Here I am, Mrs. Collins," and waits until she is told what to do. They both have a cup of coffee while they plan her day's work.

"What'll I do now?" is perhaps the one thing that Mrs. Collins hears the most. Finding work to do for Franklin, Lyle, and Melanie gets Mrs. Collins up early and often keeps her awake. "Before I ever make a move," Mrs. Collins tells me, "the first thing I think of is Franklin and Lyle." They don't like to be idle, but they like her to tell them what to do. Mrs. Collins has never gone to some of the places she would like to, because the DeSpains take so much looking after. Especially Reuben, who can't stand to be idle now his wife is dead. This being Sunday, however, he is willing to sit in front of the barn under a new painted sign that reads

REUBEN DESPAIN

I buy junk and sell antiques

He doesn't buy junk, of course, he gets it all free, but one of his clients thought the remark would make a good sign. DeSpain came to Ordway in the early years of the Depression, when some of the whites, as well as the "coloreds," took their pay in milk and eggs and leftovers. His children wore the clothes the Collins children grew out of. He never complained. For twenty-five years he walked a horse and wagon — the horse wearing a bonnet to ward off sunstroke — up one street and down the other collecting whatever people had to throw away, or believed they had worn out. After the war it began to add up. The software, so called, Rosemary DeSpain cleaned up and sold once a year in the Methodist basement; the hardware Reuben DeSpain stowed away in the Collins barn. The government didn't want it, you couldn't eat it, or sell it, and it wouldn't burn. To make room for such stuff one of the Collins cars had to sit out in the yard, splattered with bird droppings, or in the freezing winter weather over one of the grease pits in the Collins service station. The other car, a Model T Ford with a brass radiator and a California top, had become so old it belonged in the barn as part of the junk. It had never actually been *given* to Reuben DeSpain, but, as Floyd liked to say, it had been *ceded* to him. It had been *thought* to be junk, and if it was junk it belonged to DeSpain. A gentleman in Des Moines has an option on the car, and pays five dollars a month for DeSpain to store it for him. He doesn't seem to mind that the price of the car goes up and up. Two or three times a year a woman from St. Louis comes over in her station wagon for DeSpain's old bottles, beaded lampshades, wall and mantel clocks, oil lamps, and old records. A Philadelphia firm that makes stoves will buy anything good DeSpain lays a hand on, including the old Mayflower coke burner he warms his house with over the winter. It has a "sold" tag on it, but he is free to use it while he is still around. There's more people than DeSpain can keep track of to collect the buttons he snips off old clothes. Mrs. Collins has explaned, and DeSpain has grasped, that as money gets cheaper his junk gets dearer. He lets it sit. DeSpain won't sell his records or his clocks to people who impress him as careless in such matters. Clocks run for him. Once off the premises they stop. There's an account at the bank for Reuben DeSpain and family that will pass on to his heirs if they can bother to be troubled. Money is something they don't understand, and have always left to Floyd. Besides Melanie, Franklin, and Lyle, there are Franklin's three children. In the mid-fifties Franklin, a year older than Lyle, took fifty dollars from the bank and went to Chicago where he planned a new start. He left in June and was back in October. A few years later Lyle went to St. Louis, where he enrolled in a Peace Corps program. He learned to type, and returned with a machine on which he still owed thirty-eight dollars. Both boys were noncommittal, but according to Mrs. Collins they were shocked by people's behavior. They were also homesick, and tired of people who called light-colored boys black.

Finding work for them to do was a strain for Mrs. Collins until Floyd thought of installing a car wash at the back of the service station. Running the station is a family enterprise, and all members of the family contribute to it. When Floyd was at home, he ran it; and Ruth's husband runs it in the slack season for road work; and there is always Mrs. Collins, or one of Ruth's boys, to help at the pumps on a busy weekend. The car wash occupies space once used for parking, and does a good business with college boys from Mason City. Franklin and Lyle are good workers, but they seem to lack initiative. They work better when Mrs. Collins is around, and they like her to handle the accounts. Franklin's two eldest boys are very good with a wax job, but it doesn't help matters that one has the name *Floyd*. This seemed very touching when Franklin's son was born, but it led to nothing but complications. When someone hollered "Floyd," both Floyds answered. The result was that Floyd Collins would seldom answer when his name was called. He didn't mean to be rude, or insist on *Mr.* Collins, but what could he do?

From where I am seated I can't see but I can hear the hiss and spray of steam at the car wash, and the sound of the gong as a car pulls into the station. Until just recently Reuben De-Spain took care of such things as the tires, windshields, etc., but all that stooping and bending didn't help his back any, and his right arm, especially his "windshield elbow," seemed to get worse. All he had to do was pick up a rag and he would feel the twinge of pain. Mrs. Collins thought he'd better just sit and take it easy, before it got so he couldn't use his arm to eat with. There's nothing harder for Reuben to do than just sit, but that's now what he does. His platform rocker, covered with plum-colored velvet once popular on tram seats, sits under a beach umbrella in the dappled shade at the front of the barn. The arms are too low, the back is too high, and the angle is all wrong for comfort, but DeSpain has never lost his taste for elegance. His ancestors, by published account, were influential pirates and patrons of the arts. He has the nose, forehead, and melancholy eyes of the clergy painted by El Greco. He also has the style. If DeSpain is asked if he has something or other, he will reply, "I shall endeavor to ascertain it," then go and look. For seven years he was one of the servants close to Governor Huey Long. He considers the Governor one of the country's great men. Five weeks following the assassination, DeSpain and his family, on their way to Chicago, were towed into Ordway by a Mason City milkman. The car had broken down. It proved to be an Essex, of a year and a model for which parts were no longer available. Mr. Collins let them camp in the railroad station where they could use the lavatories and the drinking fountain, while Reuben DeSpain considered his next move. That proved to be into the barn behind the Collins house. In a few weeks' time Mrs. Collins hardly knew how she had ever got along without him. "Ma'am," he said, "all Reuben DeSpain aims to do is please."

Some of the younger generation think of DeSpain as a swami, thanks to his remarkable elegance of speech. He need say no more than "Consider the lilies—" to gather a group of teen-age loafers around him. On warm sultry days, between his neck and his collar he slips a clean white kerchief scented with insect repellent. He claims it keeps him free of pests while he naps. He wears a carpenter's apron with the big nail pockets full of unsorted parking-meter pennies. He gets them from the Ordway police department. Sorting them carefully by hand, he turns up the coins he sells to a collector in Independence. Real copper pennies are so close to DeSpain's color you feel they got it from the rubbing he gives them to bring out the dates.

On weekdays you can see Franklin or Lyle seated at the barn

door tinkering with something that doesn't work. There is never an end. Just putting up the house screens and taking them down takes two or three weeks. Reuben DeSpain sits in his chair brushing off the rust with a whisk broom, his gesture that of a railroad porter dusting the lapels of Huey Long. In the winter he sits inside the barn and mends the holes. Mrs. Collins likes to feed her own chickens and collect the eggs (when there are any), but without Lyle around to milk her, the cow, Bessie, won't give her milk. In the spring the sheds need to be fumigated and the fourteen trees on the lot pruned and sprayed. In the dry spells everything has to be watered, which means dragging the hoses from faucet to faucet, the pressure sometimes getting so low it won't operate the sprinkler: Franklin's boys will have to water the tomato plants with the watering can. Both Franklin and Lyle dislike spray nozzles and prefer to stand, using their thumbs, soaking up the water with their shoes and pants legs. When a toilet bowl in the house is flushed, the pressure drops and the outside water goes off.

Inside the house the drains get clogged and water stands for days in the second-floor tub. Periodically roots close the lines to the cesspool although the nearest tree is forty-eight feet: what a root will do in its search for water defies belief. The lawn grass grows so thick right over the cesspool Mrs. Collins has to run at it with the mower, but she will not cut or use table greens from that part of the yard. Melanie has been warned not to do it, either, but somehow she forgets.

I've noticed the whole house shakes when the boys come clopping down the stairs. The pigeons kept by a neighbor, in a roost on his roof, go up on the sky like a cloud of smoke. There's always one that doesn't seem to get the swing of it, his wings flapping like a loose fan belt. Off where I can't see them, but I can hear them, Waldo and Luther are starting their horseplay. They go through the kitchen, slamming the screen, then clop around the house like cantering horses. Waldo is the one who strips the leaves off the lilac bushes as he makes the turns. These daily runs have not worn away the grass, but they have firmed it down so that it has a different color and texture, like the flattened wale of corduroy or the plush seat of a chair. Waldo is always first, a step or two ahead of Luther, and Clarence trails along like a caboose. If Luther stops suddenly, dropping to his knees, Clarence will stumble over him as if he were a bench. He never seems to learn. The green smears of grass will not wash off his elbows and bony knees. They all make about two hooting circles of the house, then Waldo heads for the clearing at the back. Where the tire swing dangles from the limb of an elm, he grasps the rope to keep from collapsing. He can't seem to stop laughing. Luther is so winded he trips on his own feet, and sprawls out on his face. He lies there giggling as if he were being tickled to death. Clarence comes along so many moments later he seems part of another scene. I first thought he had tired and run down, like a spring-wind toy. But he had merely paused to pick up a length of clothesline. He straddles Luther and flails at him with the rope — but it's too long. He can't bring it around with the proper snap. Waldo is so winded he can hardly breathe, but he hoarsely yells, "Sock it to 'im! Sock it to 'im!" Clarence tries to. The sound is that of someone beating a carpet with a small switch. Luther will not stop giggling, and Clarence cries, "I'm going to kill you! You hear me?" Waldo is still hooting, but he has sagged to drape his arms around the tire. In that position Clarence is able to flail him as if he were a slave clamped in the stocks or tied to a whipping post.

From behind the house Mrs. Collins appears holding aloft one of her leather-palmed cotton work gloves. She wags it as she comes, with loping, silent strides, to where Clarence towers over Waldo. No word is spoken. Waldo and Luther are hooting, but it appears to be a scene on silent film. All my life, or so it seems, I have watched roughhousing boys interrupted in their play by the long arm of Tom Sawyer's Aunt Polly. With a practiced gesture she grips Clarence, wheels him about, and slaps him (POWIE!) with the glove. He straightens to stand like a machine with the power switched off. From his dangling hand she takes the rope and shortens it to give him a slap across the buttocks. With a hoot, he takes off. In an instant he is followed by Waldo, who lunges to avoid the swipe she gives him. Luther is last; he goes off howling with a gleeful shriek. I hear the screen door to the kitchen open and slam, and then the clop of their feet on the front-hall stairs. The house rocks. I feel it like an earth tremor in the boards of the porch. After a bout of such horseplay all three boys like to take long showers with their clothes on, then come down and sit in the lawn swing to dry off.

Mrs. Collins stands, her face to the sky, watching the whirring flight of the neighbor's pigeons. The disturbance has flushed her face with color; she idly slaps the shortened length of rope on her thigh. "My, how we all miss Floyd!" she says, coming toward me, and her smile is that of a priestess at the close of a ceremony. She feels better, the boys feel better, and she would like to assure me I should feel better. What is a little violence in the larger ceremony of innocence? She turns to gaze toward Mr. Collins, who stands in the garden, leaning on a hand plow. His straw hat is wider than his shoulders, and the wide limp brim rests on his ears. He looks more like a boy day-dreaming at his chores than an old man resting. Nor does he move from his revery until he hears the whirring blades of the mower.

On my drive down from Chicago (I was given ten days to look into the Collins case) I stopped in St. Louis for a talk with Floyd. They're holding him there, as we say, for observation. He's a good-looking, rustically handsome boy with his mother's jaw and prominent features. I see they suit a man's face better than they do hers. He has the casual, cool manner of most young people, and lets his hair grow long at the back. While we talked he preferred to sit on the floor with his knees drawn up. Off and on he toyed with a piece of cellophane from his pack of Camel cigarettes, blowing on it softly as he held it pressed, like a blade of grass, between his thumbs. The sound emitted is high and shrill, like a trapped insect or a fingernail on glass. I once made such a sound, or tried to, blowing through a dandelion stem.

To the President of the United States Floyd Collins wrote: *I am obliged to inform you your life is threatened. I am a reasonable man. It is reason that compels me to take this action. I propose to take your one life to spare the tens of thousands of innocent men, women, and children. Please stop this war or accept the consequences.*

I liked the "please." It showed his responsible Quaker breeding and will also help to commute his sentence, since no shot was fired. During my stay in Ordway, Mrs. Collins has treated me like "one of the family," and that is how I feel. One of the family. Some, if not all, of the emotions Floyd Collins has felt. I see a cow grazing, Reuben DeSpain napping, a blue sky towers above me and green grass surrounds me, and inside the white house I hear boys at their horseplay, training to be men.

"I raised Floyd to believe anything is possible," Mrs. Collins says. As it is, of course. Here in Ordway anything is possible. Not necessarily what Mrs. Collins has in mind, or Floyd has in mind, or even the town of Ordway has in mind, but what a dream of the good life, and reasonable men, make inevitable.

*Printed September 1970 in Santa Barbara by
Noel Young for the Black Sparrow Press.
Design by Barbara Martin. This edition is
limited to 1000 copies in paper wrappers
& 200 copies handbound in boards by
Earle Gray numbered & signed by the author.*

Among Wright Morris's novels are *The Field Of Vision, Ceremony In Lone Tree,* and *One Day.* His most recent publication is *Wright Morris: A Reader,* an anthology of his writings. He and his wife make their home in Mill Valley, near San Francisco.